Time OUT!

Philomel Books
an imprint of Penguin Random House LLC
375 Hudson Street
New York, NY 10014

Copyright © 2017 by Ale Barba.
Philomel Books is a registered trademark of Penguin Random House LLC.

Library of Congress Cataloging-in-Publication Data is available upon request.

Manufactured in China by RR Donnelley Asia Printing Solutions Ltd.
ISBN 9780399163043
10 9 8 7 6 5 4 3 2 1

Edited by Jill Santopolo.
Design by Ellice M. Lee.
Text set in Cachet Std.
The art was made using acrylics and cotton paper.

Author's note: Making this book was a fantastic journey, thank you Semadar and Jill.

To Andres, Vero, and their big noses.

Some enchanted evening . . .

Ale Barba

TiME

OUT!

PHILOMEL BOOKS

That's IT!

You're in Time Out.

Stay right there until I tell
you that you can leave.

Did you hear me?

What's going on in there?

FOUR

minutes left.

I want you to
think about what
you've done.

And not **move**

a muscle!

TWO
minutes left!

I hope you're **really** thinking about it.

Okay,
**time's
up.**

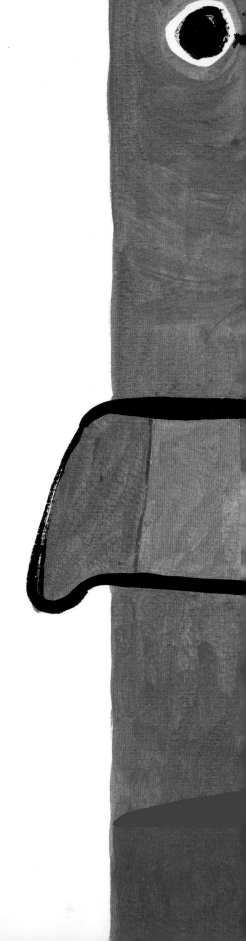

You can come out now.

You did such a good job **behaving** yourself.

Here's your
skateboard back.

TIME IN.